Anne Fine
Countdown

Crabtree Publishing Company
www.crabtreebooks.com

PMB 16A, 350 Fifth Avenue,
Suite 3308,
New York, NY 10118

616 Welland Avenue,
St. Catharines, Ontario
Canada, L2M 5V6

Fine, Anne.
Countdown / written by Anne Fine ; illustrated by Tony Trimmer.
p. cm.
Summary: Hugo can have the gerbil he wants, but only if he can first endure the boredom of spending seven hours--the length of time he is at school each day--in a nearly-empty room to learn how a caged animal feels.
ISBN-13: 978-0-7787-0958-9 (rlb)
ISBN-10: 0-7787-0958-2 (rlb)
ISBN-13: 978-0-7787-1004-2 (pbk)
ISBN-10: 0-7787-1004-1 (pbk)
[1. Boredom--Fiction. 2. Imagination--Fiction. 3. Fathers and sons--Fiction. 4. Gerbils--Fiction.] I. Trimmer, Tony, ill. II. Title.
PZ7.F495673Cou 2006
[Fic]--dc22

2005035771
LC

Published by Crabtree Publishing in 2006
First published in 2001 by Egmont Books Ltd.

Paperback ISBN 0-7787-1004-1
Reinforced Hardcover Binding ISBN 0-7787-0958-2

1 2 3 4 5 6 7 8 9 0 Printed in Italy 5 4 3 2 1 0 9 8 7 6

Anne Fine
Countdown

Illustrations by
Tony Trimmer

Yellow Bananas

To Jessie and Leah

T.T.

11:01 AM

HUGO JAMES MACFIE sat on the newspaper spread all over his empty bedroom and asked his father, “Can I have a gerbil?”

“No,” said his father, painting around the last corner.

“I promise I’d look after it properly.”

“I’m sure you would,” said his father. “But that’s not the point. Think of the gerbil. Think how you’d like to spend your whole life in a cage.”

“I’d let it out.”

“But you’re at school all day.”

Hugo counted on his fingers.

“I’m only out for seven hours.”

His father painted over the last of the yellow paint with the new blue paint.

"It's long enough to sit in a boring old cage all by yourself, with nothing to do."

"I could give it things to play with while I'm gone."

"That might not be enough to keep it happy."

"It would be clean and safe and comfy, though."

His father looked at the four freshly painted walls.

"This bedroom's clean and safe and comfy," he said. "A perfect cage, in fact, for someone your size. But you wouldn't want to spend seven hours in here, all by yourself."

"I'd be all right."

His father dropped the brush into the can. "Prove it," he said. "Spend the day here."

Hugo looked around the empty room. "The whole day?"

"Seven hours," his father said. "The time you'd usually be at school."

Hugo looked at his watch. It was eleven in the morning.

"Start at noon," said his father. "Spend the next hour getting organized, then see if you can stick it out. Midday until evening. Twelve o'clock until seven."

"And if I do it, can I have a gerbil?"

His father picked up the paint rags. "If you can do it," he said, "I'll not just bring your furniture back in. I'll bring a gerbil, too."

"Synchronize watches," said Hugo. "Make it exactly eleven-o-four."

Mr. MacFie set his watch.

"Eleven-o-four. One plate of food. One bottle of water. Three of your old toys. And all the newspaper that's spread over the floor. Is that a deal?"

"See you at twelve," said Hugo. "Ready to go."

11:58 AM

MR. MACFIE CLOSED his hand around the door knob and inspected his watch.

"Ready?"

Hugo checked everything: his water bottle here, his food plate there, and the three things he'd taken from the toybox spread out in front of him on the floor.

"Ready," he told his father. "Lock me in."

"Certainly not," said his father. "You know that's totally against my principles."

He shut the door.

12:01 PM

HUGO LOOKED AROUND what he now thought of as his nice new cage. Soft breaths of air waltzed through the open window. The one bare lightbulb hung from the matte white ceiling. The walls shone perfect Harebell Blue. Across the floor lay a square sea of newsprint. On top of that lay the three things he'd borrowed from Charlotte's toybox.

1. The dancing monkey on a stick.

2. Gray Ghostie.

3. The box of baby blocks.

He'd taken the monkey on a stick because Charlotte wouldn't let him touch it usually. He'd chosen Gray Ghostie because she was his favorite puppet when he was young. And he'd picked up the block box because he'd heard his mother say a thousand times that you could fill a child's room with expensive toys, but when it came to keeping them busy for hours and hours, you couldn't beat a box of blocks.

So. Was she right?

He built a tower.

Then he built a house.

He built a viaduct. And then a fancy archway that fell down.

And then a prison wall.

Then he was bored.

He took Gray Ghostie and made her peer over his prison wall. She looked this way and that.

"Whooooo," he made her say. "Whooooo. Whooooo. Whooooo."

Then he was bored.

He took the monkey on a stick and made it flip over and over.

"Hi, Ghostie," he made the monkey say.

"Whoooo," said Ghostie.

"Look at me."

"Whooooo."

"Backward flip. Up and over. Hanging in the air."

"Whooooo."

Gray Ghostie couldn't help sounding bored.

Hugo MacFie packed the blocks back in their box and laid the puppet ghost on top. He leaned the monkey on a stick against the lid.

As soon as he got out, he'd tell his mother she was wrong. A box of blocks was just as boring as a puppet ghost and a monkey on a stick.

How long was that, then?

Hugo studied his watch.

12:31.

Just under six and a half more hours.

12:32 PM

HE READ THE newspaper. It wasn't easy. Great splatters of paint had fallen from the ceiling, making it difficult to read. *New rules for banks* he managed to make out. Then *foreign sales on the up and up*. Boring. *Shares plunge after fears.* But fears of what was now a big white blob. He tried to pick it off, but only tore the paper.

He tried another patch.

Massive deposits . . . divided by the share price.

Boring.

He crawled across the floor, nose to the paper. There it was, all around him: business news. Nothing worth reading. No *KILLER SHARK EATS FAMILY OF FOUR*. No *WIND SNATCHES WIG OFF BEAUTY QUEEN*. No *MORE HAUNTED HOUSE HORRORS - See pages 4-11*. When he grew up, he'd buy a great newspaper, not the *Financial Times*. He'd speak to his father about it the moment he got out of here.

When would that be?

Hugo looked at his watch.

In six hours and twenty-one minutes.

Less than an hour gone. It seemed like *weeks*.

12:42 PM

SO WAS HE hungry yet? Hugo thought for a minute. He wasn't hungry yet. He'd had a big breakfast. Then, just in case, an early lunch. His orange sat on the plate. His sandwich waited. And his three chocolate cookies lay in a pile. He planned to eat his snack at four-thirty. Then, when he got out at seven, he'd have the supper his mother promised to keep warm.

That was the plan. He studied the plate again. Orange. Sandwich. And two chocolate cookies. Hugo stared. Where had the third one *gone?*

Guiltily, he brushed the cookie crumbs off his chest. He hadn't even noticed he was eating it.

Only 12:44.

What a *waste.*

If he'd been thinking properly, he'd have taken more time.

12:47 PM

HUGO ROCKED GENTLY backward and forward on the floor. The walls swayed with him, blue as sky. Sky all around. No, *sea*. Sea all around him. He was on a raft. A speckled, printed raft. The blobs of paint were droppings from the gulls. No land in sight. Nothing but sea for miles and miles. Perhaps a dolphin would come. Maybe a whale. Or even sharks. What was that strange shape over there that looked like a paint scraper on the floor, but could as easily be . . .

Shark!

Sending the sandwich flying, Hugo snatched up the plate and paddled with all his might.

"Save me!" he whispered frantically through gritted teeth. "Oh, save me, someone! Is there no one there?"

Around him, the seagulls cried. The lightbulb sun beat down. And the soft zephyrs crept over the sill, over the waves and raft, cooling his fevered brow.

He paddled desperately.

"Oh, for a sight of land! Six weeks! Six desperate weeks adrift. My stores so low that I have only a sandwich, an orange, and two ship's cookies left. If no vessel passes, I shall surely die!"

His paddling grew more frantic.

"Help!" he cried. "Help me! – Oh, oh, help!"

But no help came.

Hugo paddled onward through the waves until, discouraged and exhausted, he lost hope, and ate his only sandwich.

12:59 PM

NATURALLY, AS A man will, stuck on an ocean on a raft, he soon went crazy.

"Ghostie," he whispered. "Ghostie, can you remember back when you were mine?"

Ghostie nodded. How could she forget?

"And you were white?"

Forlornly, Ghostie hung her head.

"Well," Hugo confessed. "You know that day Mom stuffed you in the washing machine by mistake, and I sat and watched you going around and around, until you went gray?"

Ghostie nodded again.

"That was my fault," admitted Hugo. "I was the one who dropped you in the laundry basket by mistake. If I'd done what I was told, and sorted the laundry more carefully, you wouldn't have gone all lumpy and gray."

Ghostie hung her lumpy head.

"Sorry," said Hugo. "I am really sorry."

Ghostie said not a word.

"Still," Hugo said, cheering suddenly. "I feel a whole lot better, just for telling you."

Ghostie stared.

1:03 PM

HUGO LEANED OUT of the window as far as he dared. If he could slip his hand around the metal strut holding the gutter up, then he could swing across to the drainpipe. Then he could shimmy down that as far as the tree, and, if the big branch held, he could slide down to Mr. Foster's wall, crawl along that, and let himself down on the garbage bins.

Or he could rip his clothes into long shreds and knot them tightly together, like a rope, and tie it to the window latch. Then he could slither down and jump, trying to make sure he missed the rosebush, and land on the grass, next to the cat's bowl.

Or he could climb up on the eavestroughs, balance along and then crawl up the roof, over the top, and down the other side, on to the porch.

Or he could just walk out the door, of course . . .

But not for – he studied his watch – five hours and fifty minutes.

He watched the numbers on his watch face flash and change.

Five hours and forty-nine minutes.

He watched them change again.

Five hours and forty-eight minutes.

A gerbil wouldn't have a watch, of course, to countdown the minutes. All that a gerbil could do was prowl around his nice new cage.

1:13 PM

HUGO PROWLED AROUND his nice new room. The smell of paint was strongest in the corner that Dad had painted last. Sunlight fell firmly on the furthest wall, making the blue look lighter. When the sun dropped behind the tree there might be shadows he could watch to pass the time. But not until then. And that would be hours.

1:17 PM

HUGO PICKED UP the orange and tossed it in the air.

Once.

Twice.

Again.

Then, bored, he sniffed at it.

The smell of orange peel was sharper than he'd thought. He scraped with his nail to make it smell even more strongly, then he laid down and held the orange to his nose.

Now he was lying underneath an orange tree. He was in Spain. If he opened his eyes he'd see the terrace and the swimming pool. He'd inch his way across the burning tiles and slither over the edge, into the crystal water. The cooling blue would close over his head and he would twist and turn under the sunlit droplets.

Splash, splash!

Free as a fish!

No. He was an eagle now. From way, way up, he'd spot the orange peeking from its branch, and swoop down, from sheer high spirits, to knock it from the tree. The sharp fizz taste would smear his beak and send him wheeling up again, into high skies.

Flap, flap!

Free as a bird!

1:26.

But he was here, under a matte white ceiling, trapped in on all four sides by Harebell Blue walls. Beneath him lapped, not silken water, but the grubby old *Financial Times*.

On vacation, his father said, a dozen times a day, "This is the life!"

And this, thought Hugo, definitely wasn't.

1:29 PM

FIRST HE RIPPED out the word *HELP.* (He found it in a headline: *HELP FOR SALES.*) Then he tore gently around the *ME* (in *MERCHANDISE*). He found an *I* (in *INTEREST RATES*), an *AM* (in *AMERICAN SHARES*), the letters *TRA* (in *TRADE FIGURES*), a spare *P* (in *PENSIONS*), and then a *PED* (in *PEDESTRIAN PRECINCT*).

He found the thickest blob of paint (just above

SCOTTISH WORKFORCE SLASHED) and picked it off. It was still sticky, luckily. He used it to glue his message to the blankest patch of paper he could find (which was a bit of bare wall in the photo of the Manager of a grocery store).

His fingers were covered with matte white, but he'd done it.

What did he need now?

An empty bottle, of course.

Hugo tipped back his head and drank his water, every drop of it. He rolled his message up and pushed it in. Then he crawled to the door.

Footsteps!

He definitely heard them coming up the stairs. Was it his mom? Or his dad? It couldn't be Charlotte. She was still at Grandma's house. He put his ear to the door.

Thud, thud.

His heart beat with excitement.

Thud, thud, thud.

The steps drew nearer. Then they passed the door. He heard a rattle further along the landing. Someone was going into his parents' bedroom now. It could be either of them. Hard to tell.

He waited, his ear pressed up against the door, for quite a while. And then he heard the whole performance again, but in reverse.

Rattle.

Then *thud, thud, thud* along the landing – *right* outside his door!

Then *thud, thud,* down the stairs, fading away.

Hugo leaned back against the door, exhausted from the excitement.

It was the most dramatic thing that had happened in – Hugo studied his watch – nearly two hours.

1:56.

1:59 PM

"Okay," HUGO TOLD his brain firmly. "Stop thinking. Empty yourself. Go blank. Go totally blank."

Right at the back of his brain, a silent voice reminded him sharply:

"Let's not forget our manners. Try saying 'please'."

"Please," Hugo thought to himself. And then he wondered why he felt obliged to suck up to one small bit of him. "You wouldn't say 'please' to a toenail, would you? Or to a knee? Why should your brain get all the fancy treatment?" Was it fair?

Hugo tried unsaying "please."

"I didn't mean that," Hugo told his brain. "It doesn't count. We're starting off again."

He took a deep breath.

"Okay," he said. "Stop thinking. Empty yourself. Go totally blank."

"You mind your manners, Hugo," said his brain.

"My manners are none of your business."

"I think they are," his brain said loftily.

"Who says?"

"I do."

"But you're just me. You're nothing but my brain. And if it weren't for me, you wouldn't be here, would you?"

"And if it weren't for me," his brain said nastily, "you wouldn't be here either. So snubs to you."

"And snubs to you."

"With big brass knobs on."

"And with double return."

Hugo jumped to his feet.

"I'm going crazy!" he said aloud.

"Serves you right!" crowed his brain.

"Shut up!"

"Shut up yourself."

"You shut up first."

"No, *you*."

"You started it."

"I certainly did not."

And Hugo knew his brain was right. He'd started it himself by trying to tell his brain what it should do.

"Truce?" offered Hugo.

"Truce," agreed his brain.

It took a bit of time and both the chocolate cookies, but in the end the brain piped down in Hugo's head.

By 2:09, he felt himself again.

2:13 PM

HUGO SANG *Flower of Scotland* to the lightbulb at the top of his voice. Then he sang *When my Sugar Walked Down the Street* (his father's favorite), then a short medley from the book of nursery rhymes he'd been forced to pass down to Charlotte. Then he sang television jingles. Then the theme song from *The Flintstones.* Then the first verse – all that he could remember – of Grandma's favorite hymn: *The Head That Once Was Crowned With Thorns.*

Then he sang *Flower of Scotland* all over again. Then he was bored, and sat twiddling his thumbs, waiting for the end number to change on his watch face.

2:30; 2:31; 2:32.

He lost track of time for a bit – 2:37, then tried, unsuccessfully, to pick the last of the sticky white paint off his fingertips. Then he

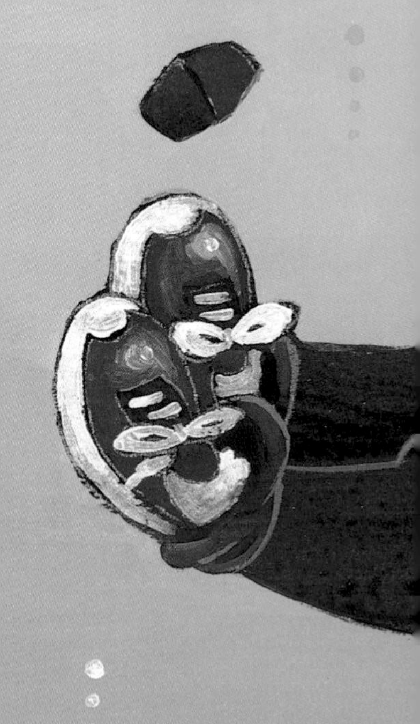

laid back and imagined himself drowning. Down, down into the salty darkness he would go, through all the folding billows of the sea, his hair rippling like weeds, his eyes ablaze like underwater headlamps.

He sat up and looked at his watch.

2:41.

2:43 PM

HUGO JAMES MACFIE took a quick vote on it. The monkey on a stick was all for giving up at once. Gray Ghostie was happy either way. And Hugo didn't give the blocks a say.

The lightbulb stared down dispassionately as Hugo announced the official result.

"In favor of staying: none. In favor of leaving: two."

That was settled then. They were leaving. Hugo picked up his two companions (abandoning the blocks) and walked to the door. He checked his watch face as he opened it.

2:47

He bumped into his father on the stairs. His father looked at him. Then he looked at Hugo's fingertips.

"I hope you haven't left sticky white fingerprints all over my freshly painted walls," he said.

Hugo ignored him.

Mr. MacFie gave his son another long, steady look. "Would you like me to help you carry your stuff back in?" he asked.

Hugo shook his head firmly. "No, thank you," he told his father. "Not right now. I thought I'd go outside and play."

"A wise decision," said his father gravely.

He stood and watched as Hugo James MacFie went down the stairs and out of the front door, into the wind and sun.

2:49 PM — THE END.

Other titles in the Yellow Banana bunch:

Amina's Blanket
A Break in the Chain
Colly's Bard
Dragon Trouble
Fine Feathered Friend
Jo-Jo- the Melon Donkey
The Monster from Underground
My Brother Bernadette
Soccer Star
Stranger from Somewhere in Time
Who's a Clever Girl?
Snakes and Ladders
Long Gray Norris
Dracula's Daughter